To Dear Uanna
with love from
the neighbours
2016

MARGARET MAHY · GAVIN BISHOP
· MISTER WHISTLER ·

GECKO PRESS

Mister Whistler woke up kicking his feet in the air.
His sheets were twined and tangled around him,
and his room was full of echoes. He'd been singing
and dancing in his sleep.

Then the phone rang.

"This is your Great-Aunt Lydia Whistler. Listen, Whistler, I can't see anything through my smeary windows. I wish you'd come over and clean them for me—right away!"

Mister Whistler sighed. Such a lively song was singing itself in his head. His twitching feet were longing to dance.

But he put on his blue spotted underpants, his neat blue trousers, and his undershirt.

He put on a clean ironed shirt, a waistcoat, a jacket, and a big green coat with a fur collar. Last of all he clapped his hat on his head.

He went to the station and bought a ticket to Whistlestop.

"Now, think carefully," he told himself. The song in his head was
making him scatterbrained. "Have I washed my face? Yes!
Did I brush my teeth? Yes!
Am I neatly dressed? Yes! Neat as a pin.
Have I got my ticket? Yes! It's here in my hand.
Do I have a nice clean freshly ironed handkerchief?
Let me check."

All the time, the song raced round and round his head, and his
feet tried to dance him round and round the platform.

Mister Whistler slid his ticket between his fine, white, freshly brushed teeth. He felt in his big coat pockets.

Right? No! Left? No! Top left? Ah! Good!

His handkerchief was safely folded in his top left pocket.
But...but...

Mister Whistler patted himself wildly.

He felt again in the bottom pockets of his big coat.
He felt in his top pocket. Nothing there but the handkerchief.

No ticket!

"Must be in my jacket," he thought.
He danced his way out of his coat so he could
feel in his jacket pockets.

Nothing in the top pockets except a twenty-cent piece and a ballpoint pen. Nothing in the bottom pockets except a piece of string and a button.

Mister Whistler tap danced impatiently.

"Perhaps I slipped it into my waistcoat?" he thought.

It was hard to reach his waistcoat pockets so he danced his way out of his jacket, folded it neatly, and dropped it onto his coat.

Nothing in the right pocket. Nothing in the left.

The song kept singing in Mister Whistler's head.

"I know! I must have put it in my shirt pocket."

Mister Whistler's waistcoat fitted so snugly it was hard to reach his shirt pocket. Swish! He whisked his waistcoat off, folding it neatly as he danced, and laid it delicately down on his jacket and coat.

He poked his fingers into the little
top pockets of his shirt.

Nothing in the right pocket.
Nothing in the left.

"Oh, I'm a fool," thought Mister Whistler.
"It will be in my trouser pocket."

He felt in his right pocket.
He felt in his left.

Nothing.

Quickly, quickly!

Mister Whistler spun in wild circles, keeping time with the music in his head.

Nothing! Nothing!

No, wait! There was something!
His left-hand pocket had a hole in it.

"Oh no!" thought Mister Whistler.
"My ticket's fallen through the hole.
It's worked its way down into my trousers."

Mister Whistler danced out of his trousers.

People gasped at his elegant spotted underpants and his clean undershirt.
But he was too busy turning his trousers inside out to notice.

Nothing!

He turned the trousers upside down and shook them.

No ticket!

Nothing!

Mister Whistler clapped his hands to his head in dancing despair.

"My hat!" he suddenly thought. "Of course! I've put my ticket in my hatband." He took off his hat but the hatband was empty.

Mister Whistler danced with fury, tossing his hat onto the pile of clothes.

Suddenly people were
clapping and cheering.

"What dancing!" they cried.
"What energy! What grace!"

Mister Whistler looked around.
People began dropping
money into his hat.

"I've lost my ticket!" Mister Whistler wailed. And as he wailed, something flew out from between his teeth and fluttered like a butterfly to the ground.

"My ticket!" Mister Whistler yelled. He scooped up the ticket and kissed it. "But I must dress. Great-Aunt Lydia will be furious if I turn up in my underwear."

For dressing, he needed both hands.

Again, he slid the ticket between his fine, strong teeth.

Into his trousers!
Quickly! Quickly!

Into his shirt!
Quickly!

Into his waistcoat! Into his jacket!
Quickly! Quickly! Quickly!

Into his big coat.
Hurry!

Then he picked up his hat. It was overflowing with money! He poured the money into his coat pockets and made a deep bow. Everyone cheered and clapped as he ran for the train and leaped gracefully aboard.

All was well! Mister Whistler was dressed again.
He was on the train. But oh dear...where was his ticket?

It was in his mouth, safely clenched between his teeth.

Mister Whistler laughed.

His ticket flapped like a mad moth to the back of his mouth.
Mister Whistler choked and swallowed.

He swallowed his ticket.

Mister Whistler had to buy a new ticket when the guard came around.

Wasn't it a lucky thing he'd earned all that money with his wild dancing?

This edition first published in 2013 by Gecko Press,
PO Box 9335, Marion Square, Wellington 6141, New Zealand.
info@geckopress.com. Reprinted 2013, twice.

Distributed in New Zealand by Random House NZ
Distributed in Australia by Scholastic Australia
Distributed in the United Kingdom by Bounce Sales & Marketing

First American edition published in 2013 by Gecko Press USA, an imprint of Gecko Press Ltd. Distributed in the
United States and Canada by Lerner Publishing Group, Inc. 241 First Avenue North, Minneapolis, MN, 55401 USA
www.lernerbooks.com

A catalog record for this book is available from the US Library of Congress.

A catalogue record for this book is available from the National Library of New Zealand.

 Gecko Press acknowledges the generous support of
Creative New Zealand.

Design by Spencer Levine, Wellington, New Zealand
Printed by Everbest, China
ISBN hardback: 978-1-877467-91-2 • ISBN paperback: 978-1-877467-92-9

For more curiously good books, visit www.geckopress.com